Ladybird Readers

The Pony Games

Series Editor: Sorrel Pitts

Adapted by Sorrel Pitts

LADYBIRD BOOKS

UK | USA | Canada | Ireland | Australia
India | New Zealand | South Africa

Ladybird Books is part of the Penguin Random House group of companies
whose addresses can be found at global.penguinrandomhouse.com.
www.penguin.co.uk   www.puffin.co.uk   www.ladybird.co.uk

Penguin
Random House
UK

First published by Ladybird Books Ltd, 2018
001

HASBRO and its logo, MY LITTLE PONY and all related characters are trademarks of Hasbro
and are used with permission.
© 2018 Hasbro. All rights reserved.

Licensed by:

Printed in China

A CIP catalogue record for this book is available from the British Library

ISBN: 978–0–241–31956–7

All correspondence to
Ladybird Books
Penguin Random House Children's
80 Strand, London WC2R 0RL

MIX
Paper from
responsible sources
FSC® C018179

Ladybird Readers

The Pony Games

Picture words

Rainbow
Dash

Bulk
Biceps

Twilight
Sparkle

Fluttershy

Rarity

Applejack

Fleetfoot

Soarin

Spitfire

Wonderbolt
team

Ponyville
team

teams

apple pies

rainbow

guidebook

beads

Rainbow Dash was talking to Fluttershy and Bulk Biceps. Rainbow Dash was excited.

"It's the Pony Games in Rainbow Falls next week, and we've been invited!" said Rainbow Dash.

"We're in the Ponyville team, and we're going to fly in the most important race! So, we have to practice," she said.

So, the ponies began practicing. They flew up into the air—and fell down on Rainbow Dash!

"This isn't going to be easy," said Rainbow Dash.

A few days later, Rainbow Dash and Twilight Sparkle met the Wonderbolt ponies on the train. They were all traveling to the Pony Games.

"Good luck, Rainbow Dash!" the Wonderbolt team said.

"Thank you for flying in the Ponyville team," Twilight Sparkle said to Rainbow Dash. "I know the Wonderbolt ponies are faster than us."

"We are all very happy because we are racing for Ponyville," said Fluttershy. "I'm sure that we can win if we practice."

Rarity and Applejack were on the train, too.

"I'm going to buy some Pony Games clothes!" Rarity said. "Our team's clothes will be the best!"

"The Ponyville ponies must buy my apple pies," said Applejack. "Then, they will be warm and happy while they watch the race!"

That afternoon, the ponies arrived in Rainbow Falls.

"Wow!" they said. "Look at all the colors in the rainbows!"

Twilight Sparkle decided to look around Rainbow Falls. She was reading her guidebook while she walked.

Rainbow Falls has a very
long river. The town was built
next to the river. Together,
the water and sun make lots
of rainbows.

"Rainbow Falls has a big market, where ponies sell lots of things for the Pony Games," said Twilight Sparkle.

Then, Twilight met Pinkie Pie and Rarity.

"I'm shopping for Pony Games clothes," said Rarity.

Twilight, Rarity, and Pinkie Pie visited the market together.

"I can buy some beautiful beads here," said Rarity. "They will be perfect on my Pony Games clothes."

"Get your warm apple pies here!" called Applejack.

Lots of ponies came to buy her pies.

Back at the Pony Games, the Wonderbolt team's fastest pony, Soarin, was practicing hard for the big race.

Suddenly, Soarin fell, but Rainbow Dash flew through the air to save him! She carried him safely down to the ground.

"Thank you for saving me, Rainbow Dash," said Soarin.

"Oh, Rainbow Dash, you are wonderful," said Fluttershy. "You carried Soarin down from the sky."

"Soarin, are you OK?" asked Fluttershy.

"My wing hurts," Soarin said. "I need to rest it, but I'm sure it will be OK for the race."

Soarin's wing wasn't OK, and he had to go to the hospital.
The Wonderbolt team's fastest pony was hurt, and he couldn't fly.

"We must ask Rainbow Dash
to fly with us!" said Spitfire.

The Wonderbolt ponies went to speak to Rainbow Dash.

"Do you want to practice with us while Soarin is in the hospital?" asked Fleetfoot.

"Oh . . . no, thank you," Rainbow Dash answered quickly. "I'm flying with the Ponyville team. We're going to practice now."

"Are you sure? We're the fastest team," said Spitfire.

Rainbow Dash thought for a moment. She wanted to fly with the fastest ponies.

"OK, I'll do it," she said, "but just for a few hours . . ."

So, Rainbow Dash practiced with the Wonderbolt ponies. She flew high, and she flew low. She flew in, out, and around!

Rainbow Dash saw Bulk Biceps and Fluttershy. They were practicing, too.

"Come on, Bulk Biceps. You can do it!" Fluttershy was shouting.

The next day, Twilight spoke to Rainbow Dash.

"Practicing with two teams isn't easy," Twilight said.

Rainbow Dash was very surprised. "You know about the Wonderbolt ponies!" she replied.

"If you fly in the Wonderbolt team, then the Ponyville team won't race," said Twilight. "The ponies won't see Rarity's clothes, or eat Applejack's apple pies."

"What shall I do?"
asked Rainbow Dash.

"You must decide," said Twilight,
"but the race is tomorrow, so
decide soon."

"We can't win if Rainbow Dash doesn't fly with us," said Applejack. "Then, what will I do with all these apple pies?"

"What will I do with all these clothes?" asked Rarity.

Rainbow Dash knew what to do. She spoke to the two teams.

"Listen to me, everyone," she said. "I want to race with the Ponyville team, because my friends need me more."

The Ponyville team was
very happy.

"Come on, team, let's practice!"
said Rainbow Dash.

It was time for the race.

All the Ponyville ponies were there. They wore Rarity's Pony Games clothes, and they ate Applejack's apple pies. They were very excited.

The race started.

The Wonderbolt team flew well,
but Fluttershy, Bulk Biceps,
and Rainbow Dash flew higher
and faster.

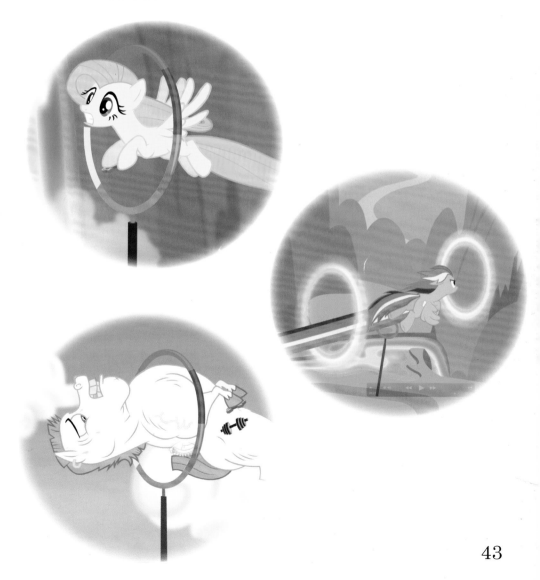

The Ponyville team won!

"It's always nice to win," said Rainbow Dash, "but I've learned that friends are more important than winning."

"After today, my friends will always come first," she said.

Activities

The key below describes the skills practiced in each activity.

Spelling and writing

Reading

Speaking

Critical thinking

Preparation for the Cambridge Young Learners exams

1 Circle the correct words.

1 Rainbow Dash was talking to Fluttershy and **Rarity. /Bulk Biceps.**

2 "It's the Pony Games in Rainbow Falls next week," said **Rainbow Dash. / Fluttershy.**

3 "We're in the Ponyville **team," / race,"** said Rainbow Dash.

4 "We're going to fly in the most important **rainbow!" / race!"**

2 **Match the two parts of the sentences. Then, write them on the lines.**

1 The ponies began

a be easy," said Rainbow Dash.

2 They flew up

b practicing.

3 "This isn't going to

c into the air.

1 The ponies began practicing.

2

3

3 **Who said this?**

Rainbow Dash   Applejack   Rarity   Twilight Sparkle

1 "This isn't going to be easy," said

Rainbow Dash .

2 "The Wonderbolt ponies are faster than us," said

.

3 "I'm going to buy some Pony Games clothes," said

.

4 "The Ponyville ponies must buy my apple pies," said

.

4 Ask and answer the questions with a friend. 🗨

1 *Who went to Rainbow Falls on the train?*

The Ponyville team and the Wonderbolt team went to Rainbow Falls on the train.

2 Which team is faster, the Ponyville team or the Wonderbolt team?

3 What must the Ponyville team do if they want to win?

5 **Look and read. Write *T* (true) or *F* (false).**

1 Twilight Sparkle looked around Rainbow Falls.   T

2 Twilight Sparkle was flying and reading at the same time.

3 Rainbow Falls was built next to a river.

4 Together, the water and sun make lots of rain.

6 **Choose the correct answers.**

That afternoon, the ponies arrived in Rainbow Falls.

"Wow!" they said. "Look at all the colors in the rainbows!"

1 How did the ponies travel to Rainbow Falls?

   a by plane   **b** by train

2 When did the ponies arrive in Rainbow Falls?

   a in the morning   **b** in the afternoon

3 What did the ponies see when they arrived?

   a rainbows   **b** rain

4 What did the ponies enjoy seeing?

   a all the trees   **b** all the colors

7 Do the crossword.

Across

1 This pony fell from the sky.

3 Rainbow Falls has a long . . .

5 Rarity wanted to buy these.

Down

2 There were lots of these at Rainbow Falls.

4 Ponyville ponies wanted to watch this.

8 Write the missing letters.

ai ea ui

1  t ea m

2  tr_____n

3  g_____debook

4  r_____nbow

5  b_____ds

9 **Look and read. Put a** ✓ **or a** ✗ **in the boxes.** 📖 ❇️ ❓

1 Rarity went to the market to buy clothes for the Ponyville ponies. ✓

2 Rarity bought beads to make her new Pony Games clothes look more beautiful. ☐

3 Twilight Sparkle wasn't interested in new places. ☐

4 The ponies were hungry, so Applejack gave them all some bread. ☐

10 **Read, and write the correct form of the verbs.** 📖 ✏️

Back at the Pony Games, the Wonderbolt team's fastest pony, Soarin, ¹ <u>was practicing</u> (**practice**) hard for the big race.

Suddenly, Soarin ² _____ (**fall**), but Rainbow Dash ³ _____ (**fly**) through the air to save him!

She ⁴ _____ (**carry**) him safely down to the ground. "Thank you for ⁵ _____ (**save**) me, Rainbow Dash," said Soarin.

11 **Read the questions. Write answers using words in the box.**

> important race   faster than
>
> want to race with

1 Why did Rainbow Dash want to race in the Pony Games?

The Ponyville team was going to fly in the most important race.

2 What did Twilight Sparkle know about the Wonderbolt team?

_____

_____

3 What did Twilight Sparkle mean when she said, "Practicing with two teams isn't easy."?

_____

_____

12 **Answer the questions.**

1 Why did Rainbow Dash practice with the Wonderbolt team?
Because she wanted to fly with the fastest ponies.

2 What did Fluttershy shout at Bulk Biceps?

3 What did Twilight speak to Rainbow Dash about?

4 How did Rainbow Dash feel?

13 Talk to a friend about Rainbow Dash. Answer the questions. 💬 🗨

1
> *What did Rainbow Dash have to decide?*

> *She had to decide which team to fly with.*

2 Why did the Ponyville team want Rainbow Dash to fly with them?

3 What did Rainbow Dash decide to do?

4 What did Rainbow Dash learn?

14 Order the story. Write 1—4.

.... Rainbow Dash decided to race with the Ponyville team, not the Wonderbolt team.

___1___ Rainbow Dash and the Ponyville team were invited to race in the Pony Games.

.... Soarin was hurt, so Rainbow Dash also practiced with the Wonderbolt team.

.... The Ponyville team won the race.

15 **Circle the correct sentences.**

1 **a** The Wonderbolt team flew higher and faster than the Ponyville team.

b The Ponyville team flew higher and faster than the Wonderbolt team.

2 **a** The Pony Games won!

b The Ponyville team won!

3 **a** After today, Rainbow Dash's friends will always come first.

b After today, Rainbow Dash's friends will never come first.

16 Read the sentences. Choose the correct words and write them on the lines. 📖 ✏️ ⭐

---

1 to watch   watch   watching

2 lost   won   watch

3 and   that   which

4 come to me   come last   come first

---

1 All the Ponyville ponies came ___to watch___ the big race.

2 The Ponyville team _____!

3 "It's always nice to win, but I've learned _____ friends are more important than winning."

4 "After today, my friends will always _____."

17 Write about your favorite pony in the story. Why is he or she your favorite? ✏️ ❓

My favorite pony is

Level 4

The Pied Piper of Hamelin

978-0-241-25378-6 ☐

The Wizard of Oz

978-0-241-25379-3 ☐

Sam and the Robots

978-0-241-25380-9 ☐

The Little Mermaid

978-0-241-29874-9 ☐

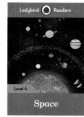

Space

978-0-241-25381-6 ☐

Pinocchio

978-0-241-28430-8 ☐

Alice in Wonderland

978-0-241-28431-5 ☐

Under the Oceans

978-0-241-29888-6 ☐

Knights and Castles

978-0-241-28432-2 ☐

Heidi

978-0-241-28433-9 ☐

Peter and the Wolf

978-0-241-28434-6 ☐

Dangerous Journeys

978-0-241-29891-6 ☐

A Fight with Underbite

978-0-241-29890-9 ☐

Sideswipe Loses his Head

978-0-241-29889-3 ☐

Aladdin

978-0-241-31606-1 ☐

Forests

978-0-241-31958-1 ☐

The Pony Games

978-0-241-31956-7 ☐